THE DANCING STARS

AN IROQUOIS LEGEND

retold and illustrated

by

Anne Rockwell

Thomas Y. Crowell Company
New York

A NOTE ABOUT THE STORY

When the stars we call the Pleiades appeared in the autumn sky, the Iroquois Indians of four or five centuries ago knew it was time to gather in their harvest and make ready for the cold weather to come. Later, in their long-houses in the winter evenings they retold the age-old tales of the origin of the universe, among them, this story of the dancing stars.

It seems natural that the Iroquois envisioned seven brothers dancing up to the sky, for the members of this tribe are notably fleet. Some of them have been great long-distance runners, and many others are so surefooted that they are in great demand as construction workers on the high steel frames of skyscrapers.

Manufactured in the United States of America

L.C. Card 76-171008
ISBN 0-690-23176-8   0-690-23177-6(LB)
1   2   3   4   5   6   7   8   9   10

For Hannah, Elizabeth, and Oliver

Once upon a time, when the earth and sky were new, there lived seven little brothers. They loved to play and dance in the forest, and no matter where they went, they always went there together.

One evening at twilight as they were returning to their longhouse from the forest, they heard from far, far away the sound of someone singing.

The song was not like any song they had ever heard before. It was so beautiful and mysterious the seven brothers completely forgot about going home. Instead they danced off in the direction of the song.

As the little boys danced, their feet seemed to grow lighter. Suddenly night came. Then, before long, they could see the forest and the great longhouses of their people stretched out far below them in the moonlight. They saw that they were dancing right up in the sky.

Higher and higher they danced, and the song grew louder. Still higher they danced, and the song grew louder and sweeter still.

"I came," sang the sweet voice, "for a
hunter pursued me, and now I am lost
in the sky. But sleep, my little ones,
in your warm dark cave. I will watch
over you here in the sky."

Then the brothers saw a great black bear. She had a long tail made of stars, and she wore a necklace and belt made of white and shining clamshells.

Stars twinkled at her nose and her toes,
and the clamshells, too, sparkled like
bright stars.

It was she who was singing the lullaby
the boys had heard, and they danced
closer to her.

The great bear's lullaby was beautiful, and they danced a long time to it. But at last they wanted to go home, for it was very late, but they did not remember the way. They begged the moon to show them how to go back to their longhouse, but the moon only smiled and said:

"This is your home now, my children.
We welcome you, I and the stars, for we
enjoy watching you dance."

And the boys went on dancing, and strangely enough, they found that they did not grow tired at all.

The bear's song grew louder and sweeter.
Behind each boy a bright star grew, and
the moon smiled at their dance.

Then the smallest star boy heard a tiny voice from far away. Someone was crying and calling his name. Over the sound of the bear's song and of his brothers' dancing feet he listened, and he heard the distant voice again.

It was his mother's voice.

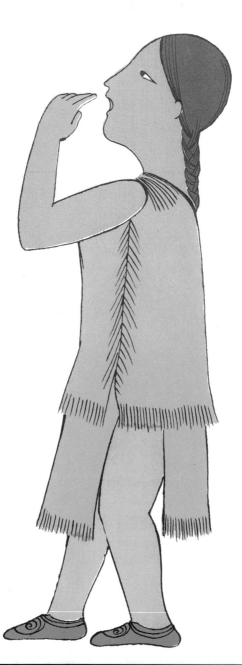

The smallest boy began to run as fast as he could go, with the bright star he was wearing making a shining trail behind him.

"Come back, come back," cried his brothers and the moon, but the little boy raced away from them.

Down he flew,

past the eagle's nest,

past the clouds,

and closer and closer to the
earth, as the sound of his mother calling
him grew louder and louder.

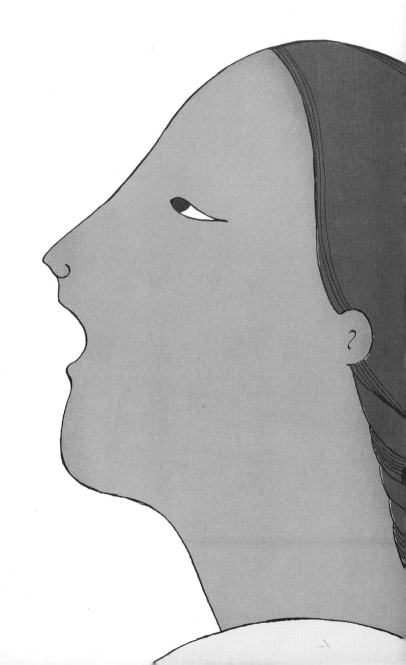

Soon he could see her. She could almost
touch his hand.

Then he landed on the earth.

But where he landed there was no boy. There was only a hole, the kind a star makes when it falls. His mother cried still harder when she saw the fallen star. Then she looked up and saw her other boys dancing in the sky.

"Stay there. Stay there," she called to them over the great bear's song, for she did not want them to fall, too.

They heard her, as they danced far away and high in the sky, and they nodded their heads to show her they would obey.

The mother wept for the fallen star, and where her warm tears fell, a little green shoot sprang up.

Higher and higher the green shoot grew.

It was the smallest brother reaching for
the sky, so he could be with his brothers
again.

Higher and higher it grew, until it reached
the place where the brothers danced and
the great bear sang.

"Welcome, dear brother," said the dancing star boys to the tall pine tree who had come to join them.

The pine tree is still there, the tallest tree in the forest. And you can see the brothers dancing even now, in the night sky, while the great bear sings her little bears to sleep.